HEARTBEATS IN INK

A Poetry Collection

Denise Alicea

DEDICATION

Thank you to my friends and family
for your unwavering support.

"Love will find a way through paths where wolves fear to prey."
— Lord Byron

CONTENTS

FALLING IN LOVE

Falling in love, a feeling so grand,
A whirlwind of emotions, us, hand in hand.
My heart beating fast, my breath catching deep.
Oh, I'm drawn to you, my love, my sweet, sweet keep.
Your smile lights my world, your eyes so bright,
I'm lost in your gaze, each day, each night.
Your touch, so gentle, your kiss, so sweet.
My heart skips a beat each time our worlds meet.
I'm falling for you, deeper and deeper,
My love for you growing, steeper and steeper.
You're my everything, my one true love,
Sent directly from above, a gift from the dove.
Oh, the joy of falling in love!
A feeling so pure, a blessing from above.
My heart is yours, forever and always,
To cherish and to hold, through all the crazy days.
This to say, I'm falling for you, my love, my dear,
And I'll love you forever, my one and only, my greatest cheer.

THE HEART'S SYMPHONY

In the depths of my chest,
Where love resides,
My heart beats with a fervor,
One like the ocean's tides.
When you're near,
My heart skips a beat,
A tender dance of ecstasy,
So sweet and all complete.
In your eyes, I see my destiny,
A love always pure and true,
Which sets my heart free.
Oh, my love,
You're the reason I sing.
My heart beats for you,
My love for you is truly everything.

Love's Enduring Embrace

In whispers soft, like morning dew,
Love's tendrils reach out, theirs a tender hue.
A gentle touch, a gaze that holds,
A story spun in hearts untold.
Through sunlit fields and moonlit lanes,
It dances light, erases all pains.
A symphony in every beat,
Two souls entwined, their rhythm sweet.

In laughter shared, in tears that fall,
Love's tapestry embraces all.
A fortress built on trust and grace,
A haven found in each embrace.

With every sunrise, hope takes flight,
Love's embers glow, theirs a guiding light.
Through storms, Love braves with constant flame,
A whispered promise, a whispered name.

For Love's a bridge across the years,
A whispered promise, drying all tears.
A silent vow, forever true,
A love that sings for me and you.

MOONLIT PAWS

In eyes of gold, a sunlit gleam,
A purring hum, a whispered dream.
Soft paws that tread on moonlit floors.
A brush of fur, then silence, more.
A flick of tail, a knowing gaze.
In shadows deep, a hunter's maze.
A velvet warmth, a rumbling sigh,
A love that speaks without any lie.
No need for words, no grand display,
In every touch, sweet words they say.
A bond that lives in stolen naps,
In gentle nudges, the softest taps.
So raise a paw, a grateful meow
For the feline friends who love us now.
In purring peace, in playful grace,
Their love's a gift, in every space.

COSMIC LOVE

In the velvet cloak of night, they gleam,
A cosmic dance, a celestial dream.
Above, a tapestry of tales untold.
In that vast expanse, their secrets unfold.

Twinkling diamonds in the inky abyss,
Each star, a promise, a true, tender kiss.
They shimmer and sigh, a silent art,
A symphony of love from the very start.

Upon the canvas of the midnight sky,
They etch tales of a love that will never die.
A cosmic ballet, a timeless romance,
Where hearts align in cosmic dance.

The moon, a witness to love's refrain,
As constellations echo a lover's name.
Far beyond earthly cares and earthly fears,
Love whispers soft in cosmic ears.

In that vastness, where galaxies swirl,
Love too unfurls like a luminous pearl.
A dance of passion, a celestial rhyme,
As souls entwine across space, across time.

Oh, the stars, each a single beacon of light,
Guiding lovers through the tranquil night.

A cosmic connection, one pure and divine,
In that vastness vast universe, our love will shine.

Gaze upon the heavens, eyes aglow,
As the stars above, their love bestow.
Our love, a starlit symphony.
Something celestial for all to see.

HOPE

In shadows deep, where doubts reside,
A flicker glows, a hope implied.
A light that dances, steadfast, true,
Through storms and sorrows, it sees us through.

Hope, the ember, in darkest night,
Steadfast, unwavering, burning so bright.
It stitches wounds, paints futures clear,
A beacon that guides, that dispels fear.

In whispered echoes, troubled minds,
Hope's melody that solace finds.
A symphony of grace and scope.
Yes, in every heartbeat, thrives our hope.

THOUGHTS OF YOU

Beneath the moon's soft, muted light,
Whispers of you move through the night.
Memories play their gentle tunes,
An orchestra beneath the moon.

In the quiet, shadows yearn
For your gaze, a love discerned.
Absence paints the world in blue.
Well, in every shade, I'm missing you.

Still, hope persists, a steady stream,
That fate will bridge the space between.
Until our paths entwine once more,
I'll treasure the love we had before.

SELF-LOVE HARMONY

In the heart's quiet chambers, a melody sings,
Self-love, a symphony, the new beginnings it brings.

Acceptance blooms like petals in a sacred space,
A masterpiece unfolding, all flaws embraced.

Mirror, reflect the love within that's true,
A celebration of self, a dance, a clue.

You're a universe, a treasure trove of worth.
No need for approval from external girth!

Whisper kindness, let compassion, let the self lead,
In self-love's garden, tend to every seed.

Embrace scars as stories, wounds will find their balm,
Their healing journey, their eternally soothing psalm.

So dance to your heart's rhythm, its work of art,
Its masterpiece of love. Here, joy finds its start.

ENDURING LOVE

Not a fire's blaze, but an ember's glow, Love that weathers winter's cold blows. Hands entwined, though seasons turn, Roots that, in each other, yearn.

Whispers soft in twilight's hush, A laugh, now shared, a gentle brush. Eyes that speak with depths untold. Stories, in each wrinkle, bold.

Sunsets painted, hand in hand, Footprints etched in shifting sand. Through storm and calm, our souls entwine, A tapestry, our love, divine.

WOVEN THREADS

Two paths that weave, not twist apart,
Through laughter's bloom and shadows' art.
A silent language, shared and known,
In glances warm, a seed, sown.

Secrets whispered, tears unseen.
Shoulders strong, a steady lean.
Victories danced, defeats embraced,
A fortress built, so no storm is erased.

Time's tapestry unspools its thread
In memories sewn, forever fed.
Though miles may stretch or years may roam,
Friendship's flame will always find home.

DESTINY

In starlit whispers, threads are spun,
A tapestry of lives just recently begun,
Where paths unseen begin to bend,
And destiny writes the open end.

Is it a force unseen, untamed?
A hand that throws the dice we've named?
Echoes of a whispered prayer?
A guide of whispers through the air?

Perhaps it's woven in the soul,
A compass pointing toward a goal,
A flame which burns with hidden might,
Leading us through dark and light.

But free will dances in the breeze,
A butterfly on swaying trees,
Each choice, a thread we intertwine,
A beautiful weaving of what could be mine.

Walk with open eyes,
Embrace the stumble and the rise,
For destiny, though etched in stars
Is shaped by choices, both near and far.
With every turn, we write our names,
Our own whispers echo in the game
Of love and loss and dreams that soar,
The symphony of what we've always been born for.

Trust the dance, the ebb and flow,
The whispered secrets softly grow,
In every breath, in every beat,
Our destiny, a song complete.

CASTLE IN THE SKY

With clouds as cobblestones and stardust for grout, A castle in the sky, a whispered doubt. Its ramparts reach for heavens wide, where whispers of wishes on moonbeams ride.

No mortar, no stone, by wind, all is held, In tapestries woven, stories are spelled. Of dragons that dance in aurora's embrace, Mermaids who sing with the ocean's soft grace.

Through halls of starlight, whispers take flight, Of dreams yet to bloom, bathed in silver light. A haven for those with hearts light, free, where laughter floats wild on the great celestial sea.

But beware, dear traveler, of the shadows that creep, Where doubts take their form, the secrets they keep. For castles in dreams can be fragile and fair, and wishes untamed can turn easily to despair.

Yet still, it stands tall, a beacon so bright, A reminder to chase stars through endless night. For even in whispers, dreams hold the key, to unlock the magic which sets us both free.

Let your heart soar on wings of the breeze, And dance with the shadows in starlit trees. For the castle in the sky, though ever so high, may be just the bridge to the dreams in your eye.

MY LOVE

With you, my love, the world feels newly spun, A tapestry of secrets, found one by one. Each glance, a whisper lost in laughter's spray, each touch, a map to landscapes not on public display.

Your eyes, uncharted galaxies, I roam, discovering constellations, calling them my new home. Your skin, a whispered parchment, safe and untorn, where hidden tales in freckles are newly born.

We trace the lines of smiles, uncharted shores, Unravel mysteries and whispers nevermore. Your laugh, a sunrise on an unknown coast, Paints dawn on beaches where our souls heal the most.

With every beat, a treasure coming to light, Hidden within the rhythm of night. Your breath, a starlit map, a guiding spark, To lead us deeper through dark.

In every kiss, a hidden continent, where lips collide in languages unspent. We build our empires, brick by stolen sigh, a kingdom forged in dreams that touch the sky.

With you, my love, the world's a chase, an endless quest for wonders, one we embrace. So let us wander, hand in hand, and find the secrets tucked in your heart, your mind.

For in your depths, I lose and win the greatest prize: to love and start again.

POWER OF LOVE

Love's a whisper in the breeze,
A gentle touch which sets the soul at ease.
It's a sunrise painting skies with gold,
A story whispered, never to grow old.
Love's a fortress, strong and tall,
A refuge for the weary, home, they call.
A river carving through stone,
A steady current, never to be alone.
Love's a dance beneath moonlit sky,
A secret language, only hearts can spy.
It's a melody that fills the air,
A symphony of joy, dispelling all cares.
Love's a fire that burns within,
A warmth which chases out bitter sin.
It's a light that guides us through the night,
A beacon shining strong and bright.
Love's a seed which takes its root
And blossoms to branches, bearing sweet fruit.
So let us cherish love's tight embrace,
This precious gift, a sacred space.
For in its depths, we find our way,
To live and laugh, to love another day.

LOVING LIFE

Life, a vibrant, elaborate thread,
Moment's dance, joy widespread.
Dreams flutter like butterflies,
Colors swirling in the skies.

In laughter, tears mend,
Love for life, an endless trend.
Raise a toast! To here and now!
A heartfelt ode to life's most sacred vow.

MAKING WAVES

In the realm of change, where dreams are spun,
A whisper to a roar, a battle won.
In the heart of stillness, a spark ignites,
A revolution born in darkest nights.

Ripples in the water, a pebble's embrace,
Start a wave of courage, a transformative chase.
From shores of silence to depths profound,
Change emerges, a symphony unbound.

With every step, a journey unfolds,
Breaking barriers, stories still untold.
A canvas painted with colors so bright.
Change, the artist, in the soft moonlight.

Casting stones of hope across the sea
In order to create waves of possibility.
The echoes of courage, the echoes of might,
A tapestry woven in the fabric of the night.

Stand on the shoreline, feel the power surge,
As waves of change begin to emerge.
A movement, a dance, an eternal flow,
In the heartbeat of progress, let it grow.

Together, we stand. United, we stride,
Creating waves which cannot be denied.
For change is a song, a melody untamed,
A symphony of voices, eternally proclaimed.

HAPPINESS

Beneath the sun's warm, golden ray,
In joy's embrace, we find our way.
Smiles bloom like flowers in spring,
Heart's melody, happiness to sweetly sing.

Laughter dances to a carefree tune,
Beneath the large and tranquil moon.
Chasing worries, they fade away.
In happiness, we choose to stay.

Sunshine hues in sky so blue,
Painting a canvas, a joyful view.
In each moment, let joy reside,
For happiness is life's closest guide.

BOLD WOMAN

In the tapestry of courage, a tale unfolds
Of a woman bold, whose spirit never molds.
She walks with grace, a fierce flame aglow
In the garden of strength that continues to grow.

Her eyes hold stories, reflections of fire,
A burning desire that will never truly tire.
Fearless in the face of the great unknown,
A warrior's heart in a world she'll own.

In every step, a declaration rings,
A melody of strength, an anthem she sings.
With conviction in her stride,
She conquers all, a fearless guide.

A bold woman, a force untamed,
Her essence, a beacon, cannot be truly named.
She paints the sky with hues of gold,
A symphony of courage, bold, vastness foretold.

Her words, like echoes, resonate,
Breaking barriers, defying fate.
In the dance of life, she takes the lead,
A tapestry of courage, woven with speed.

Bold and unyielding, she stands tall,
A testament to resilience, a daring call.
In the book of time, her chapters unfold,
A story of triumph; a woman bold.

CRUSH

In the garden of whispers, a secret unfolds,
Where petals of passion, my heart withholds.
A flutter of butterflies, a dance in the air,
A tale of a crush, beyond compare.

Eyes like galaxies, sparkling, bright,
Igniting a flame, even in depths of night.
A smile that paints my canvas of dreams,
A symphony of emotions, silent, it seems.

In the realm of daydreams, where fantasies bloom,
A secret garden, a sweet, fragrant perfume.
Heartbeats in rhythm, a melody so new,
A crush's enchantment, a love that grew.

Words unspoken, yet language so clear,
Whispers of longing, drawing ever nearer.
Each stolen glance, a chapter untold,
In the story of a crush, one pure, one bold.

A blush like roses in morning light,
A magnetic pull, an irresistible sight.
In the tapestry of emotions, colors flush,
A masterpiece painted with hues of a crush.

Oh, the magic of the moments when our eyes meet,
A serendipitous dance, so tender and sweet.
In the diary of feelings, a chapter still to hush,
The tale of a heart, tangled in a crush.

WONDER

Beneath the canopy of the starry night,
In the quiet where true dreams take flight.
A world of wonder, where mysteries unfold.
In the tapestry of existence, there are stories untold.

A child's gaze, wide-eyed, bright,
Captivated by the wonders of the dark, dark night.
Stars like diamonds, a celestial array,
A cosmic dance, a vast, perfect ballet.

Mountains standing tall, so ancient, so grand,
Whispers of wonder in the shifting sand.
Oceans stretch, boundless and deep,
A universe of other secrets, waiting to seep.

In the meadows where wildflowers bloom,
Wonder unfurls, dispelling all gloom.
The symphony of nature, a harmonious song,
In every rustle, in each breeze, wonder continues to throng.

The dance of seasons, a cyclical embrace,
A perpetual wonder in time and space.
In every question, in every ponder,
A journey embarked on the wings of wonder.

For wonder is the spark for the creative soul,
A perpetual flame, an eternal goal.
In the vast expanse where dreams unfurl:
Wonder, the compass in life's grand swirl.

ROSE

In the garden's embrace, a rose unfolds,
Its crimson petals, the story it holds.
Silken tendrils, such delicate grace,
Love's language in each small trace.

Thorns stand guard, a paradoxical blend,
Nature's sonnet, eternal verses penned.
Raindrops on petals, like tears of morn.
In twilight's embrace, love is always reborn.

LEGACY

In the tapestry of time, echoes reside,
Ancestral whispers, their timeless guides.
Roots run deep, through earth and sky,
Legacy's embrace, never passing by.

In the veins of history, a resilient flow,
Lessons learned in the ebb and glow.
Faces unknown, yet spirits entwine,
A lineage of strength, heritage so divine.

Through trials faced and battles won,
Courage of past, glistening in morning sun.
In the dance of shadows, stories unfold,
A saga of endurance, a narrative bold.

Whispers of struggle, whispers of grace,
Ancestors' presence in every cast space.
Their dreams and hopes, a flame that glows,
In the heart's alcove, reverence still grows.

Ancestral tapestry, woven with care,
Threads of resilience, love in the air.
In the symphony of time, a timeless play,
The ancestors' legacy lights our way.

STANDING TALL

In shadows deep, where challenges rise,
A spirit strong, with determined eyes.
Bearing the weight of adversity's call,
A tale unfolds of one standing tall.

In the tempest's roar, with stones that roll,
A beacon of resilience, a steadfast soul.
Through trials and tribulations, they stride,
Facing the storm, with unwavering pride.

Mountains may rise, obstacles may loom,
Yet, undeterred, one dispels the gloom.
Like a sturdy oak in the tempest's might,
Roots embedded deep, firm and tight.

Adversity's fire may fiercely burn,
Yet within, a flame of persistence continues to churn.
For in the crucible of challenge and strife,
Emerges the strength that defines a life.

Stand tall, a tower of the truest grace.
In the tapestry of time, please, leave your trace.
For in every trial, a lesson to glean.
When standing tall, you become a living dream.

MEMORIES

In the album of time, pages turned with years
Lie memories cherished, like precious souvenirs.
A tapestry woven with threads of life past,
Each moment a gem, eternity to last.

Whispers of laughter, echoes of delight,
In corridors of memory, dancing oh so bright.
Faces and places, like stars in dark night,
A constellation of moments, a celestial light.

Childhood's innocence, a garden of play,
Footprints on beaches, where oceans hold sway.
Sunsets paint the sky's canvas, so vast,
A kaleidoscope of memories, spellbound and cast.

The fragrance of rain on a warm summer's eve
Or the warmth of a hug, the solace it weaves.
First steps, first words, a journey begun.
In the mosaic of memories, a tale is spun.

Time may elapse, like a river's cool flow,
Yet memories linger in eternal glow.
Fading, not with seasons, nor ever with the tide.
In the heart's treasury, they forever abide.

Faces may age, and landscapes may change,
But memories endure, they rearrange.

A gallery of moments, a lifelong melody,
Each memory a note, in grand symphony.

Hold dear, each memory's kind embrace,
For in them lies the beauty of life's true grace.
A memoir written in joy, sorrow, glee,
A timeless ode to the dance of memory.

SYMPATHY

In the quiet realm where empathy resides,
A gentle current of compassion guides.
Sympathy, yes a balm for the heart,
A tender salve, where healing may start.

In the echo of tears, a shared refrain,
A language unspoken, not ever in vain.
A bridge of understanding, compassion's key,
In sacred spaces where hearts agree.

For in sympathy's embrace, we easily find
A solace that eases the troubled mind.
It's the silent language of a caring gaze,
The presence that lingers through somber days.

When shadows loom and burdens weigh,
Sympathy whispers, "You're not alone today."
A shared moment, connection profound,
The symphony of life, such a harmonious sound.

Be vessels of sympathy's gravity and grace,
An anchor in all storms life may embrace.
For in understanding, compassion's decree,
We become threads in a blanket of empathy.

CHOICES

In life's tapestry of choices spun,
Threads of fate, a tale begun.
Crossroads echo destiny's song.
Heart's compass guides, right or wrong.

Garden of choices, blooms diverse,
Dance with fate, in every sole verse.
Labyrinth of chances, that we weave,
Kaleidoscopes, many paths to believe.

Embrace the power, courage decides
In chaos, in all chaos, beauty resides.
Pen of choice, writes life's song,
A masterpiece in choices strong.

PEACE

In tranquil fields, sunlight gleams.
A gentle breeze, like whispers, teems.
The world finds solace in such a hush,
A peaceful scene, a tranquil blush.

Mountains stand with heads held high,
Beneath the serene, azure, cool sky.
Rivers flow with calming grace
And reflect the tranquility of such embrace.

In hearts that harbor no disdain,
empathy and love still do remain.
Peace blooms like a tender flower,
In every quiet, secluded hour.

No echoes of discord, no room for strife,
Just harmony weaving through this life.
Let peace be the anthem that we sing,
A melody which makes the world take wing.

TRANQUILITY

In the stillness of dawn's embrace,
whispers weave through silent space.
Tranquility, a gentle stream,
Reflecting dreams in moonlight's gleam.

The world in hush, a calm repose,
A symphony where true serenity flows.
Nature's brush paints skies in hues,
Soft lullabies are their kindest muse.

Mountains stand in tranquil might,
Guardians of peaceful night.
Meadows sigh their tranquil sighs,
As breezes dance, clouds wander by.

A tranquil pond, a mirror clear,
Captures stars that twinkle near.
Ripples form in quiet grace,
As they reflect both time and space.

In solitude, a tranquil heart,
Finds solace in each quiet part.
A sanctuary, an inner sea,
Where waves of peace flow endlessly.

Let tranquility be your purest guide.
In tranquil spaces, let joy reside.
Embrace the calm, let worries cease
In tranquil arms of sweet release.

I WILL BELIEVE

I will believe in hope's bright light,
Its beacon through the darkest night.
Through shadows deep and trials old,
In hope's embrace, my heart takes firm hold.

I will believe when storms arise
That hope persists and never dies.
A resilient flame that cannot fade.
In every trial, it's there to aid.

I will believe when skies are gray,
That hope will paint a brighter day.
In hope's anthem, a steadfast song,
I'll find the strength to carry on.

I will believe when doubts arise
That hope's a spark that never lies.
With unwavering faith, I'll perceive
The miracles hope can weave.

I will believe in tomorrow's dawn.
In hope's embrace, I will be drawn.
For in believing, we find our way
To brighter, hopeful, more beautiful days.

A PLACE AT THE TABLE

At the table of life, a place is set,
For every soul, no one to forget.
A gathering of hearts, diverse, wide,
A celebration of unity, all side-by-side.

No matter the color, the creed, the name,
All are welcome, no one carrying blame.
A seat for the dreamer with visions bold,
Whose stories of hope and courage are told.

The laughter of children, pure and free,
Echoes around, like waves in the sea.
Old and young, hand-in-hand,
In this shared moment, together we stand.

A chair for the weary, burdened with strife,
Finds comfort in the warmth of our life.
And next to them, the optimist's cheer,
Whispering, "In unity, there's truly none to fear."

No exclusion, no judgment's gaze,
Just open arms, accepting ways.
A mosaic of stories, a tapestry of grace.
At this table, all will find their true space.

For kindness and love are the dishes we share.
In this banquet of life, everyone cares.
A promise of togetherness, strong and stable,
A forever invitation, yes, your place at each table.

STAY

In shadows deep, where moonlight weaves,
A whisper lingers among all leaves.
My heart, a melody in soft array
Beckons each night for you to stay.

In tender moments, time takes flight,
Embraced by stars and celestial light.
Your presence, a gentle, soothing ray.
My heart implores, "Oh, won't you stay?"

Through the ebb of time, my yearning plea
Echoes of love, my symphony.
Like petals dancing in the breeze,
My heart soars high, with hopes to please.

Oh, linger here, in sweet refrain.
Let love's gentle rhythm, our hearts sustain.
For, in this moment, come what may.
My heart, dear one, will implore you stay.

Love is Never Lost

In time's tapestry, love weaves its thread,
A bond unbroken where hearts are led.
Through the seasons that come and go,
Love's flame persists, an eternal, warm glow.

In the dance of fate, where paths may part,
Love lingers onward, a work of art.
Though distance may try to claim its cost,
Love transcends, never truly lost.

In whispered winds and moonlit skies,
Love echoes in each heartfelt sigh.
For every tear that may be shed,
Love remains, a band unwed.

Through trials and storms, it stands all tests,
A sanctuary, nestled in the heart's nest.
In time's tapestry, yes, woven and tossed,
Love endures, never truly lost.

ABOUT THE AUTHOR

 Born in Manhattan and raised in Connecticut, Denise Alicea started writing when drawing and painting simply weren't enough to articulate everything she needed to say. A writer of poetry, romance, and children's books, Denise has won two awards for her short stories and has received several finalist nominations. She loves technology, reading, watching movies, and managing her blog over at The Pen & Muse Book Reviews.

Website: http://denisealicea.com

Book Blog: http://thepenmuse.net

Join the newsletter:
https://www.subscribepage.com/z7p0o9

www.ingramcontent.com/pod-product-compliance
Lightning Source LLC
Chambersburg PA
CBHW070811120626

46557CB00002B/820